For you are fearfully and wonderfully made...

PSALMS 139

On the Night You Were Born

Nancy Tillman

FEIWEL AND FRIENDS

New York

On the night you were born,
the moon smiled with such wonder
that the stars peeked in to see you
and the night wind whispered,
"Life will never be the same."

Because there had never been anyone like you...
ever in the world.

So enchanted with you were the wind and the rain
that they whispered the sound of your wonderful name.

The sound of your name is a magical one.
Let's say it out loud before we go on.

It sailed through the farmland
high on the breeze...

Over the ocean...

And through the trees...

Until everyone heard it
and everyone knew
of the one and only ever you.

Not once had there been such eyes,
such a nose,
such silly, wiggly, wonderful toes.

In fact, I think I'll count to three
so you can wiggle your toes for me.

When the polar bears heard,
they danced until dawn.

From faraway places,
the geese flew home.

The moon stayed up until morning next day.

And none of the ladybugs flew away.

So whenever you doubt just how special you are
and you wonder who loves you, how much and how far,
listen for geese honking high in the sky.
(They're singing a song to remember you by.)

Or notice the bears asleep at the zoo.
(It's because they've been dancing all night for you!)

Or drift off to sleep to the sound of the wind.
(Listen closely...it's whispering your name again!)

If the moon stays up until morning one day,
or a ladybug lands and decides to stay,
or a little bird sits at your window awhile,
it's because they're all hoping to see you smile...

For never before in story or rhyme

(not even once upon a time)

has the world ever known a you, my friend,

and it never will, not ever again...

Heaven blew every trumpet
and played every horn
on the wonderful, marvelous
night you were born.

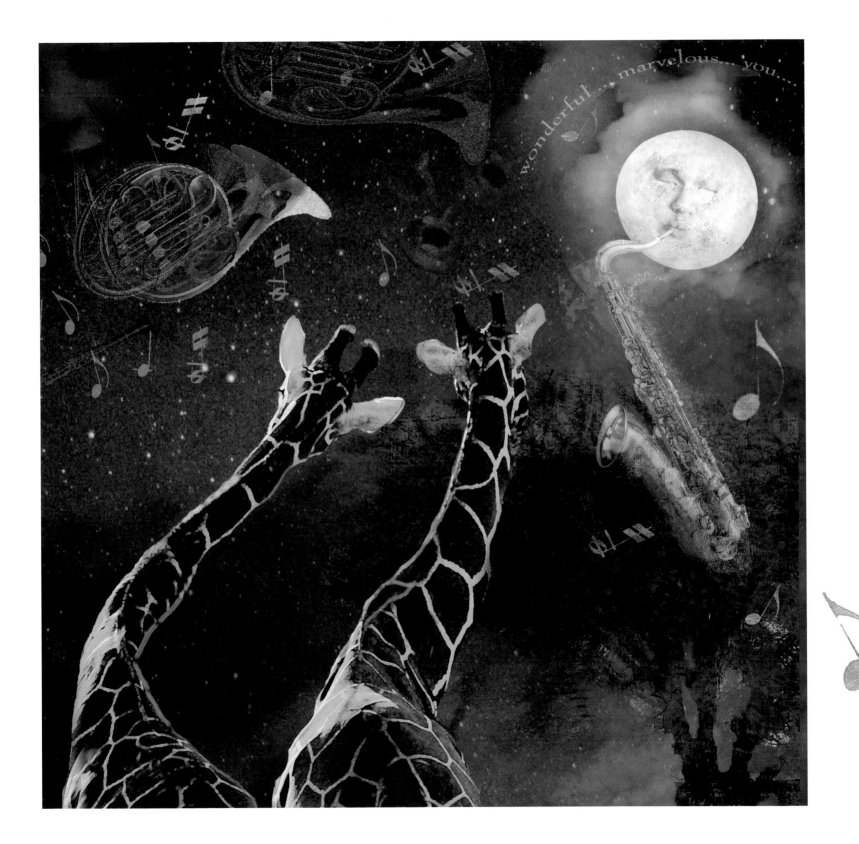

To Tucker and Tess, who are fearfully and wonderfully made.

A Feiwel and Friends Book
An Imprint of Macmillan

On the Night You Were Born. Copyright © 2005 by Nancy Tillman. All rights reserved.
Printed in June 2011 in China by South China Printing Co. Ltd., Dongguan City, Guangdong Province.
For information, address Feiwel and Friends, 175 Fifth Avenue, New York, N.Y. 10010.

Library of Congress Cataloging-in-Publication Data available

ISBN: 978-1-250-00292-1

Feiwel and Friends logo designed by Filomena Tuosto
First published in the United States by Darling Press LLC

First Feiwel and Friends Edition: 2006

10 9 8 7 6 5 4 3 2 1
mackids.com

Nancy Tillman is the author and illustrator of the bestselling picture book *Wherever You Are, My Love Will Find You;*
as well as *The Wonder of You: A Book for Celebrating Baby's First Year; The Spirit of Christmas;*
It's Time to Sleep, My Love (with Eric Metaxas); *The Crown on Your Head;* and *Tumford the Terrible.*

Nancy's mission in creating her books is to convey to children everywhere that "You are loved." She lives in Portland, Oregon.
You can visit her on the Web at www.nancytillman.com.

This special edition was printed for Kohl's Department Stores, Inc. (for distribution on behalf
of Kohl's Cares, LLC, its wholly owned subsidiary) by Feiwel and Friends.
978-1-250-00292-1 • Kohl's • 1-250-00292-3 • 123386 • 6/11–10/11

You are loved.